Books by Matt Christopher

Sports Stories
The Lucky Baseball Bat
Baseball Pals
Basketball Sparkplug
Little Lefty
Touchdown for Tommy
Break for the Basket
Baseball Flyhawk
Catcher with a Glass Arm
The Counterfeit Tackle
Miracle at the Plate
The Year Mom Won the
    Pennant
The Basket Counts
Catch That Pass!
Shortstop from Tokyo
Jackrabbit Goalie
The Fox Steals Home
Johnny Long Legs
Look Who's Playing First
    Base
Tough to Tackle
The Kid Who Only Hit
    Homers
Face-Off
Mystery Coach
Ice Magic
No Arm in Left Field
Jinx Glove
Front Court Hex
The Team That Stopped
    Moving
Glue Fingers

The Pigeon with the
    Tennis Elbow
The Submarine Pitch
Power Play
Football Fugitive
Johnny No Hit
Soccer Halfback
Diamond Champs
Dirt Bike Racer
The Dog That Called
    the Signals
The Dog That Stole
    Football Plays
Drag-Strip Racer
Run, Billy, Run
Tight End
The Twenty-one Mile
    Swim
Wild Pitch
Dirt Bike Runaway
The Great Quarterback
    Switch
Supercharged
    Infield
The Hockey Machine
Red-Hot Hightops

Animal Stories
Desperate Search
Stranded
Earthquake
Devil Pony

Ice Magic

ICE MAGIC

Matt Christopher

Illustrated by Byron Goto

Little, Brown and Company
BOSTON · NEW YORK · TORONTO · LONDON

Library of Congress Cataloging in Publication Data
Christopher, Matthew F.
  Ice magic.

  Summary: The twins' toy hockey game seems to be magic as it plays
games identical to the real ones before they even happen.
  [1. Hockey—Stories] I. Goto, Byron   illus.
II. Title.
PZ7.C458Ic   [Fic]   73-4885
ISBN 0-316-13958-0
ISBN 0-316-13991-2 (pbk.)

HC: 10 9 8 7
 PB: 15 14

VB
*Published simultaneously in Canada
by Little, Brown & Company (Canada) Limited*

Printed in the United States of America

To Dale and Joanne

Ice Magic

1

THE MORNING of Saturday, December 1, was unlike any other morning ever in Pie Pennelli's life.

It started with a laser beam shooting at his right eye. The blinding light startled him. Then he realized that it wasn't a laser beam at all but the sun shining through a hole in the drapery of his bedroom window.

He had been dreaming.

He moved over in the bed, hating to leave its soft, velvet warmth. But he knew he would have to soon. The Fly League

hockey game started at eight o'clock and he had to be at the rink a half hour before, at the latest.

As if thinking about it was a signal, there came a sudden knocking on his door and his mother's vibrant voice. "Pie! Get up!"

"Okay," he grunted softly.

He got up, washed, put on his black and white hockey uniform and had breakfast.

"Better hustle," his mother said. "You've got only eight minutes to get to the rink." He smiled at his blond, trim mother, and as he stood up, noticed with disappointment that she was still a head taller than he was.

"I'll make it," he said, and looked at his father, a lean, broad-shouldered man with a moustache. "You going, Dad?"

5

"Can't this morning," Mr. Pennelli said. "I've got to work on the car. Who are you playing?"

"The Bears," Pie answered. "They're real good."

"So?" His father's dark brows arched. "Be better."

Pie shrugged, remembering that Dad used to say the same thing to Pat. Pie's older brother, now at State College, was one of the best defensemen in the business. It was Pat's ice skates Pie was using. They were about two sizes too large, but Dad said he couldn't afford buying a new pair. "Your feet will grow into 'em," he had told Pie.

"By then I'll be in high school," Pie had answered.

In the meantime he had to be satisfied with them, but even laced up tightly they felt like canal boats and slowed down his playing.

He flung the skates over his shoulders and went to the door. "See you later," he said, and stepped out into the bone-chilling air.

He walked up Oak Street, crossed Madison and turned left, soon reaching the high wire fence that separated the street from the gorge that gave the village of Deep Gorge its name. Just past the gorge the fence turned up at a right angle to form a protective wall between it and a path going up the steep, tree-dotted hill. A squirrel chattered as it clung, head down, onto the side of a tree that hung over the breathless chasm, and Pie smiled.

"Morning, squirrel," he nodded.

He arrived at Davis Rink and Terry — Terry "the terrible" Mason — saw him and looked up at the clock. A crooked smile came over the tall, dark-haired boy's face.

"Eight-thirty on the button," he said. "One more second and you would've been late."

Like Pie's brother, Pat, Terry also had a brother going to State College. Both Pat Pennelli and Bob Mason were competing for a position on State's hockey team.

"A second is as good as an hour," Pie snorted.

"The way you played last week I really believe it," Terry said. "What do you do Friday nights? Watch the late-late show?"

"And the late-late-late show, too," Pie replied, exasperated. He hadn't sat down yet to put on his skates and Terry was already picking on him.

Last week Terry had done the same thing, picked on him throughout the entire game. *How can I play a good game*

8

of hockey with him riding me all the time? Pie thought.

He didn't know why Terry was so crusty toward him. He wished he knew, but he didn't.

Ten minutes before game time both teams got on the ice and skated round the rink to limber up their leg muscles. The Bears wore brown uniforms with white trim and white helmets with a brown stripe across the center. Only a handful of fans sat in the stands that seated a capacity crowd of three thousand.

Up on the electric scoreboard the time clock read 12:00. The first of the four large glass buttons beneath the hour lights was lit. Each button designated a period. The game was comprised of three periods. The fourth button was lit in case of a tie score, and that was used only when the high school played.

The buzzer crashed through the sound of gliding, slithering skates. The two referees blew their whistles, and like flies both teams scrambled off the ice, leaving only their first lines.

The Penguins protected the north goal. In front of the net was goalie Ed Courtney; at right forward, Pie; at left forward, Bud Rooney; at center, Terry "the terrible" Mason; at right defense, Chuck Billings; and at left defense, Frog Alexander. Watching from behind the boards stood Coach Joe Hayes, wearing a baseball cap and yellow-rimmed glasses. Beside him sat the rest of the Penguin roster.

Phreeet! went the whistle, and the ref dropped the puck.

Terry and Ed Kadola, the Bears' belligerent center, slapped at it and it skewered across the ice to Bud. Pie sprinted down the ice, looking over his shoulder for a pass. *Slap!* Down it came as Bud shot the puck to him.

Pie hooked it with his stick, saw Terry backskate toward the Bears' net, and was about to fire the puck to him when a Bears defenseman bodychecked him. Another Bear stole the puck and slapped it hard to the other end of the ice. And Pie heard Terry yell, "You slowpoke! We could've scored!"

Almost on the heels of Terry's chaffing remark came a yell from the stands. "Come on, Pie! Show 'em!"

He didn't dare waste time looking up to see who the rooter was, but the voice sounded familiar.

Then another voice yelled his name, and this one he recognized. It was Coach Hayes. "Get down to that blue line, Pie! Hurry!"

He dug the point of his right skate into

the ice and bolted toward the line. Across the red center line the Penguins' two defensemen were struggling to wrest the puck away from the Bears' forwards. Suddenly the puck shot to the side, rammed against the boards, and bounced on its edge toward the corner.

Terry and a Bear hightailed after it. Both reached it at the same time, collided and fell. Terry, on his feet first, hooked the blade of his stick around the puck, dribbled it behind the Penguins' net, then shot it up the ice.

"Pie!" he yelled.

Pie caught the pass, turned and headed up the ice toward the Bears' net. His feet seemed to be swimming in his shoes, and he wished again that he was wearing a pair that would fit snugly. He *knew* he could skate a hundred per cent better with tighter fitting shoes.

He saw the Bears' defensemen charging toward him, and he pulled back his stick, aiming to sock the puck at the space to the right of the Bears' goaltender. *Swish!* He missed the puck completely. Then *crash!* Down he went as the two defensemen plowed into him.

Stars danced in front of his eyes as he landed on the ice, both Bears on top of him. The whistle shrilled. The Bears rolled off him, and he climbed slowly to his feet, groggy and tired.

He skated off the ice with the rest of Line 1 and felt a sharp blow against his right elbow. He turned. It was Terry, his face shining with sweat.

"Why don't you take up tumbling?" he said. "You seem to do that pretty well."

"I'll think about it," said Pie as he stomped through the open gate. He found a space on the bench and sat down.

He wasn't going to tell Terry or anyone else about his oversize skates. They'd laugh him out of the rink.

For two minutes the second lines of both teams fought but had no success in knocking the puck into the net, and for another two minutes the third lines tried unsuccessfully, too. It wasn't till the first lines went back in that a Bear broke the scoreless tie.

Then the Penguins knotted it up when Terry "the terrible" Mason, after driving down the ice from the red center line, socked the puck up into the corner of the net unassisted.

The rink resounded with a roar as jubilant Penguins drummed their sticks against the boards.

Five seconds after face-off, Pie caught a pass from Bud Rooney, bolted toward the Bears' net and saw his chance to score. The Bears' goalie had slipped to one knee at the right side of the crease and was taking his sweet old time getting to his feet.

Smack! The puck streaked like a black pellet through space. Up shot the goalie in a futile effort to catch it with his gloved hand.

Goal!

"Nice shot, Pie!" the familiar voice shouted again in the stands.

This time he recognized it, and a grin curved his lips. He looked up at the sea of faces and saw two that looked exactly alike — the Byrd twins, Jody and Joliette.

Jody waved. "See you during intermission!" he yelled.

"Can't!" Pie yelled back.

"Your fans, Pennelli?" a voice sneered near his elbow.

He turned sharply and read Terry's mocking grin.

"My friends, if you'd like to know," answered Pie and turned his attention to the game, which continued without another score to the end of the first period. Penguins 2, Bears 1.

Pie clambered off the bench and skated off the ice, plagued by his oversize shoe-skates more than he was by Terry's cutting sarcasm.

Tired and half worn out, he stepped into the locker room, sat down, and took off his helmet. The cool air felt refreshing. He was ready to settle for a few minutes of much needed rest, when in burst a couple of kids, both in blue snowsuits and both looking as alike as twins could possibly look.

"Pie!" Jody Byrd cried breathlessly.

16

"It's coming out exactly like we thought it would!"

"Exactly!" Joliette repeated.

Pie stared from one bright-eyed, red-cheeked face to the other. "What is?" he asked bewilderedly.

"The game!" Joliette cried. "It's coming out exactly the same!"

Pie frowned. "The same as what?"

Just then Terry Mason's voice cut in like a sharp-toothed saw. "Hey, you kids, beat it. Even the great Pennelli's fans aren't allowed in here."

The twins scowled at him and headed for the door. "See you after the game, Pie."

Pie nodded, still frowning. *The same as what?* he thought. *Just what were those twins talking about, anyway?*

17

2

FACE-OFF, and the second period was underway.

Terry Mason and Ed Kadola smacked at the puck. It skittered toward left forward Bud Rooney who socked it across the ice to Pie. Pie stopped it, dribbled it across the blue line, saw a Bear defenseman charging at him and passed to his right defenseman, Chuck Billings.

Bang! Chuck clouted the puck toward the Bears' net.

The Bears' goalie shifted his left leg and stopped it with his pad. He then picked it up and tossed it behind the net, where another Bear retrieved it and started to dribble it up the ice.

Crash! Pie bodychecked him at the boards as he tried to pokecheck the puck. *Phreet!* sounded a whistle, and Pie saw a ref pointing at him.

"Boarding!" the ref yelled. Pie shook his head and skated off the ice toward the penalty box.

"You went at him like a bomb," said Terry, skating up beside Pie. "You can't take more than two steps when you're checking a guy. Don't you know that?"

Pie glared at him. "I wasn't thinking about steps," he grunted. "I was thinking about getting that puck."

"Well, you'd better think about steps, too," Terry snapped.

Pie found it difficult to control his temper, and was almost pleased for the one-minute penalty. While he sat serving his sentence, the Penguins tried desperately to keep possession of the puck. They knew that if the Bears got it they could try a power play, and the Penguins, with five men on the ice instead of six, could do very little about it.

And that's what happened. A Bear stole the puck from Frog Alexander and all five of their men — the goalie remained at his position — kept control of the puck. They passed it back and forth among them, evading Bud, Terry, Chuck and Frog with quick, accurate passes.

Then *snap!* A goal!

Ed Courtney picked the puck up dejectedly and tossed it to the ref, while the huge room thundered with the resounding noise of hockey sticks drumming against the boards.

Penguins 2, Bears 2.

The ref waved Pie back onto the ice. It was a ruling that a man serving a penalty was permitted to get back into the game if the opponent scored a goal.

Ten seconds later the two-minute session was up and Line 1 skated off the ice. Line 2 accomplished nothing, but the Bears' Line 3 broke the tie when their center bombed one in from the blue line.

The Penguins' Line 1 took the ice and threatened to score over a dozen times, but the Bear goalie's fantastic saves stopped them every time.

Going into the third period Pie had his best chance of the game to chalk up a point. He had intercepted a pass from a Bear and was sprinting down the ice toward the Bears' goal with not an opponent near him.

"Score, Pie! Score!" a shout rose from the stands.

He had reached the right side of the net and was less than five feet from it. He saw the goalie crouched there like a wall, legs spread apart, the big stick on the ice in front of him. But at his right side was a clear, wide-open space, and that was where Pie hoped to direct the shot.

He had to make his move now. He had to shift quickly to the left, sweep in front of the goalie and shoot.

He shifted his skates, pointing them to the left in front of the crease in the direction he wanted to go. Then something happened. His feet had turned, and so had his skates. But not far enough. The combination of oversize shoes and momentum made it impossible for Pie to turn in time, and he went crashing into the goalie.

The whistle shrilled. Disgruntled, he disentangled himself from the goalie and

crawled out of the crease. He wasn't hurt, but he couldn't tell whether the goalie was. The face mask hid any sign that might be on the guy's face.

But it didn't hide the look in the guy's eyes, the sparks of anger shooting from them.

"I'm sorry," Pie said apologetically.

He saw the ref pointing at him and then at the penalty box. "Charging!" the man in the striped shirt announced.

And once again Pie had to serve a one-minute sentence.

"You had it made, man!" yelled Terry. "And you blew it!"

You would have blown it too if you were in my shoes, Pie wanted to tell him.

Again the Bears used a power play to take advantage of the six men against five on the ice, and again they scored.

Pie came back on the ice filled with the determination to get that score back, and he managed to drive a shot that missed the net by inches. He could skate reasonably well forward, backward, and to the left and right, and he wouldn't commit a foul or lose his balance as long as he didn't attempt any sudden turns. But Pie knew that he had to make fast moves to score and that those sudden turns would always be his pitfall.

The two minutes were up and Line 2 came in. Center Rusty Carr scored with an assist by left forward Bob Taylor at 9:17 on the clock, then scored again unassisted. Penguins 4, Bears 4.

Line 3 failed to score but played excellent defense, keeping the Bears' third line from flashing on a single red light.

Pie, back on the ice for the second two-minute session of the period, blew another chance of scoring when Terry passed him the puck from the corner behind the Bears' net. Pie stopped the pass with the blade of his stick and started to dribble closer to the net, only to be bodychecked by a Bear and have the puck stolen from him.

"Pie!" Terry yelled. "Why didn't you shoot?"

Pie's face turned red. He realized now that he should have shot the instant he had received Terry's pass. *Man!* he thought. *I'm glad Dad isn't here to see this!*

Fifteen seconds later the Bears' Ed Kadola scored with an assist by his right forward. Then a Penguin blasted one in from the blue line to tie up the score, 5 to 5.

While the second line was on the ice, Terry said to Pie, "We're going on the ice one more time. Hope you don't do anything to get yourself in the sin bin."

"You think I *want* to get in there?" Pie snorted.

"Well — you *play* as if you do," Terry answered, bluntly.

Neither Line 2 nor Line 3 could break the tie, and Line 1 returned to the ice for its last chance. Pie remembered Terry's curt warning and tried his best not to commit a foul. He realized, though, that being careful didn't help either. Once, instead of charging toward a Bear to intercept a puck, Pie slowed down and let the man receive the pellet without trouble. Maybe, he thought — just maybe — the man might miss the puck.

He didn't. He hooked it neatly with his

stick, passed it to a teammate, and a score followed.

"Pie!" Terry shouted at him. "Why didn't you stop him?"

Ignoring him, Pie skated to his position, sullen and dead tired. *Man, I just can't do a thing right,* he thought dismally.

It was Line 2 that tied up the score again, and then Line 3 that broke it, winning the game for the Penguins 7 to 6.

They shouted joyously over their victory, and their fans cheered, too. Pie hoped that the win would make Terry forget how he had performed today. But he was sure it wouldn't. Even though Terry ignored him completely as they headed for the locker room, Pie knew that Terry never forgot someone else's mistakes — only his own.

Pie put on his shoes, slung the skates

over his shoulders, and walked out to the snow-packed street. The bright sun dazzled like a diamond through the bare trees. The frigid air nipped at his cheeks like sharp teeth.

"Hi, Pie!"

Jody and Joliette Byrd sprang from behind a bush to surprise him and laughed when he jumped.

"You crazy kids," he said. He remembered the strange comment they had made to him in the locker room immediately after the first period of the hockey game, and asked, "What were you guys saying about a game?"

"Our toy hockey game!" Jody replied, getting on Pie's left side while Joliette got on Pie's right. They both were at least a foot shorter than he, and it embarrassed him every time they greeted him this way.

Some guys had kidded him about having these little kids as friends.

But they had one thing in common with Pie which made him care less what anybody thought. It was their mutual interest in magic. Since the twins had found an old book on magic in their attic and had let Pie read it, all three of them had become so interested in the subject that they had purchased new books. Jody even said that he would become a magician when he grew up.

"And I'll be his assistant," Joliette had promised with that teeth-flashing smile of hers.

"What about the toy hockey game?" Pie asked curiously.

"Well, Jolie and I played a game last night," Jody explained. "We named the teams the Bears and the Penguins, and I had the Penguins. I also named each of the players after each of the guys on the Penguins' team."

"So?"

Jody looked at him seriously. "We played and my team won 7 to 6."

"What a coincidence," said Pie. "That was our score!"

"Right," Jody said. "But that isn't all. The guys who had scored on my team were the same ones who had scored on yours — it's like magic!"

3

PIE STARED, his mouth a small round "o." He had read a lot about magic. There was the entertaining kind in which a magician pulled doves out of his coat pockets or made a person disappear in a puff of smoke.

There were also magical spells which believers thought could make rain when crops were poor.

And there was black magic, too — in which believers thought they could hurt a victim by sticking darts into a doll which they pretended was the victim.

But this thing with the toy hockey game

was different. This was a kind of magic Pie had never read about before.

"Are you sure that all that stuff in our game really happened in yours?" he asked the twins. "Really sure?"

"Of course, we're sure," Jody replied emphatically. "Remember that last period when that Bear scored against you?"

Pie nodded. "When I let him take the puck because I was afraid I might plow into him and be called for a penalty."

"Right. Well, I had you do the same thing in our game," said Jody. "Except that I was hoping that Jolie would miss it, and I could take it from her."

Pie stared. "That's exactly what *I* had been thinking!" he cried.

The twins' expression matched his. "You had?" they asked in the same breath.

"Yes!" said Pie, and felt his nerves tingling.

They reached the junction opposite the gorge and turned right on Oak, none of them saying a word during the last one hundred feet. They were immersed in the toy hockey game which seemed to be controlled by some kind of magical power. It wasn't like anything the three had ever read about before in their lives.

"I'd like to see that game," Pie said at last. "Mind?"

"Of course not. Why don't you come over right after you change?"

"I will," said Pie. "And look — don't spill a single word about this to anybody. Not even your parents. Okay?"

Joliette laughed, "Are you kidding? They wouldn't believe it anyway! Mom thinks all that magic business is just a trick!"

"And Dad doesn't know *what* to believe!" Jody added, laughing.

Pie chuckled. "I guess our parents are very much alike," he said. "My mom and dad used to like magic when they were kids. Now they think it's kid stuff and pay no attention to it."

Pie arrived home and promised the twins he'd be over in an hour or so. They lived next door, which made their visiting each other to talk about their mutual interest — books on magic — very convenient.

"Hi, Mom," he said as he stepped into the kitchen. "What've you got to eat?"

Those were the first words he always greeted her with when he returned from a grueling hockey game. Nothing ever made him hungrier than a tough game of hockey.

"Hash browns, eggs and bacon," she said, and asked, "Who won?"

"We did. 7 to 6."

He hurried to his room, took off his uniform, showered, then dressed and returned to the kitchen. His meal was ready for him.

His mother watched him gulp it down. "Where's the fire?" she asked.

He smiled. "At Jody and Jolie's," he answered kiddingly.

After he finished he went over to the Byrds' house, and the twins invited him into the small recreation room in the basement where the toy hockey game was set up on a table. It was about eighteen inches wide and thirty-six inches long. On it stood four-inch high plywood figures that were maneuvered by rods protruding from the narrow ends. Clearly the figures were hockey players, each holding a hockey stick. Goals, made of cloth, were at both ends of the "rink."

Pie stared at it. "It looks handmade," he observed.

"It is," Jody replied. "There's a name carved on the side of it. Look."

He lifted the game and saw a crudely carved name: SKXROT. After it was a number, 1896.

"S-K-X-R-O-T," Pie read. "That's a peculiar name. 1896. That must be the date this thing was made."

"Really? Was hockey played that many years ago?" Joliette asked, incredulously.

"Oh, sure," Pie said. "It started — " He paused and stared at the date again. "That's sure funny," he said half to himself.

"What is?" Jody asked.

"I've got a copy of the *Official Hockey Guide,* and I'm sure I read that the first official ice hockey game was played in 1896!"

"Oh, man!" Jody whistled. "Weird!"

"I — I feel shivers crawling up my back," Joliette stammered, clasping her hands so tightly together the knuckles turned white.

Pie took hold of the knobs of each rod protruding from the ends of the game and began pushing them back and forth, thereby manipulating the players in the slots on the rink. A twist of the knobs one way or the other turned the players, making them hit the miniature puck.

"It's just like games you can buy in stores," Pie remarked. "Except this one is real old."

"You should've seen it when we found it," Jody said. "It was covered with dust."

A wooden, inch-high wall surrounded

39

the rink. There was a box in one corner where the score was kept. The only thing the rink lacked was a red light like the one that flashed on in a real rink when a goal was scored.

"Look at this," Jody said, handing Pie a rolled-up piece of paper that had yellowed with age. "It was wrapped around one of the rods with a rubber band."

Pie unrolled it and saw a neatly printed, four-line paragraph.

To whom it may concern: This hockey game is endowed with magical powers. However,
Beware what happens on a real rink first
Repeats here not, for fate
Promises that, as true as bubbles burst,
The magic will dissipate.

Pie read the message again, then murmured, "Hmm. This is the strangest thing I ever saw."

"Us, too," said Joliette. "And it is magic. We proved it."

"I wonder if anybody else had ever played it," Pie said.

Jody shrugged. "I don't know. It was stuck in a far corner of the attic. I wouldn't be surprised if we were the first."

"Could be," said Pie. "Well, let's play a game."

They sat at opposite sides of the game and began to play. Pie had difficulty manipulating his men as rapidly as Jody did, and after ten minutes of play Jody won, 5 to 1.

During all that time Pie looked for something strange about the toy hockey game, something that would prove to him that it definitely had magical powers. But he saw nothing, and in spite of the message that the twins had found with the game, he began to doubt its genuineness.

If he weren't so sure that the twins were sincere believers in magic, he'd think they were pulling his leg.

He was sure they were sincere, though. The expression on their faces when they had first told him about the real game was plenty of proof.

He was sure, too, that they wouldn't pull a mean trick on him about such matters. Magic to them was a real, wonderful thing, and they loved it. You don't pull practical jokes about something you love.

"May I come over before our next hockey game?" Pie asked. "I'd like to see if it'll work like the first time."

"Sure, you may," replied Jody.

"Maybe it won't work if you play it," Joliette said, her blue eyes looking at him avidly.

"Then I'll watch you guys play," Pie said.

4

O N FRIDAY Pie went next door to the Byrds' house and knocked on the door. No one answered and he knocked again. Still no one answered.

"Hi, Pie," said a voice behind him. "Aren't your little friends home?"

Pie turned and saw that it was Terry "the terrible" Mason. A calico cat was at his feet, sitting on its haunches and looking at Pie with large, yellow eyes.

"I guess they aren't," Pie said, and started off the porch.

"I heard that you and the twins are really uptight about magic," Terry said, an amused glint in his eyes. "That right?"

"That's right," agreed Pie.

Terry chuckled. "Why don't you use magic when you're on the rink? You could be the greatest."

Pie forced a smile. "Maybe I don't want to be the greatest," he said. "But I suppose *you* would."

Terry shrugged. "Why not? What's wrong with being the greatest?"

Pie considered. "Nothing, if you don't let it go to your head."

The cat at Terry's feet suddenly rose on all four paws and looked across the street. Its tail swished back and forth, and Pie looked up. What had caught the cat's attention was another cat.

Two cars were coming down the street, one behind the other, and for a moment Pie held his breath. *Does Terry see what*

44

could happen, or should I warn him? he thought.

Too late! The cat leaped off the curb and started to run across the street!

"Tipper!" Terry yelled.

There was a loud screech of tires on asphalt as the first car tried to come to a sudden stop. Then, *Bang!* The second car rammed into it.

By now Terry was running after the cat, Pie behind him. They saw it limping off the street on the other side, favoring its right hind leg. It reached the curb, lay on its side, and began licking the wounded limb.

Terry knelt beside it. "You dumb cat!" he scolded. "You want to get killed?"

Pie watched Terry take hold of the leg and stroke it gently and tenderly, and he suddenly saw a part of Terry that sur-

45

prised him. Sarcastic and humiliating though Terry was at times, he was kind and merciful to a dumb animal.

He looked up as the two drivers came running from their cars. "How's the cat?" the first man asked anxiously.

"His leg was hit," said Terry.

"Want me to take him to a vet?"

"No, thanks. I'll take care of him. He'll be all right."

"You sure?"

Terry nodded. "I'm sure."

"Okay. But watch him, will you? He might not be so lucky the next time."

They left, stopped to look at the rear of the first car, carried on a brief discussion, then got into their vehicles and drove away, waving as they went by.

"Guess neither car got damaged," Pie said.

"Glad about that," Terry replied, then turned his attention back to his cat. "You dumb cat, if I have to get a leash for you I will," he said gruffly.

He picked it up, held it close in his arms, and walked away. Pie watched. You'd think that Terry wasn't even aware that he was there.

5

AS USUAL, Pie arrived at the rink the next morning with one minute to spare. And, as usual, Terry "the terrible" Mason had a remark for him.

"Hi, early bird. Why'd you get here so soon?"

Pie ignored the sarcasm, believing that it was the best way to handle Terry. "How's your dumb cat?" he asked.

Terry shrugged. "He'll be okay. No broken bones or anything."

"Good."

Pie put on his skates and got on the rink

with the rest of the team. He wondered if the twins had played with their toy hockey game last night. He looked up at the stands but didn't see them.

He was lost in thought until the sound of the referee's whistle brought him back to reality. The ice was cleared. A second blast of the whistle brought on the first lines. The Penguins were playing the Hawks, a team wearing white helmets and green uniforms with yellow trim. Crouched opposite Terry Mason at the face-off position was the Hawks' tall center, Phil Adams.

The whistle shrilled again. The puck was dropped. Both centers sprang into action, pounding at the small black disk with short, vicious swipes. Up on the scoreboard the seconds began ticking away. 11:59 . . . 11:58 . . . 11:57 . . .

The puck turned on end and rolled into Hawk territory. Pie, the closest to it, sprinted after it. The loose fit of his shoe-skates made him glance down at the laces. They were tight, but when he looked up again a Hawk defenseman was swooping in after the puck, stick extended far forward.

They crashed into each other, their sticks striking the puck at the same time. They fought for control of it; then Pie's skate hooked the Hawk's. He lost his balance and fell.

He looked for the puck and saw it again in the Hawks' possession. He heard his name yelled and saw Terry Mason speeding by him, his eyes smoldering.

Quickly, Pie clambered to his feet and sprinted down center ice, trying to ignore Terry's flaming look. He knew what Terry was mad about. A pass to him might have meant a score. Except for the Hawks' goalie, the space between Terry and the goal had been wide open.

A pass to a Hawk at the right of the Penguins' goal was deflected by left defenseman Frog Alexander. Frog flipped it to Chuck Billings, and a wild scramble followed as the two Hawk wingmen tried to pokecheck it away from him.

"Ice it! Ice it!" yelled Coach Joe Hayes.

The Penguins weren't able to get a clear shot at the puck, and at 10:51 the Hawks scored.

They threatened again during the next minute and almost knocked in their second goal except for a great save made by goalie Ed Courtney.

"All right, first line! Off!" yelled Coach Hayes. "Get going, second line!"

Sweat beaded Pie's forehead as he skated toward the bench. He was warm but not tired, and he wished that the coach hadn't called the line off the ice so soon.

At 7:28 Brad Krupa, right forward on the Penguins' third line, sank in a fifteen-footer to tie up the score.

The first period ended with the score still knotted, 1 to 1.

It wasn't till then that Pie thought about the twins again. He looked behind him and saw several faces he recognized, including his father's and mother's. They saw him and waved, and he waved back.

He kept searching for the other pair of familiar faces — faces that looked exactly alike — but didn't see them. Something important must have happened to keep Jody and Joliette Byrd from attending the game. Had they gone somewhere last night and not returned yet? More important, had they been home long enough to have played a game on their toy ice hockey rink?

During the second period the Hawks' Phil Adams knocked in two goals, both times assisted by one of his wingmen. The Hawks had possession of the puck most of the time, and it was only because of Ed Courtney's great saves that they were not able to drive the puck into the net more often.

With the score 3 to 1 in favor of the Hawks as the teams went into the third period, Pie Pennelli was determined to make every move count, oversize shoe-skates or not. Line 1 wasn't doing as well as the other lines up to now, and that was another reason why Terry Mason was getting hot under the collar.

Terry hadn't been doing so well himself, and Pie figured it was because the irritable center had been trying to dribble the puck to the goal and shoot it in without any help. "The terrible" Mason was disgusted with his wingmen and was trying to win the game by himself. Coach Hayes warned him about it, but after exercising caution for a minute or two, Terry started playing again as if he couldn't trust his wingmen down at their end of the rink.

It was while Line 1 was on the ice for the second time during the third period that Pie struck a Hawk's leg accidentally with his stick as he tried to pokecheck the puck and was given a minute's sentence in the penalty box for tripping. He sat there, his brows heavy with sweat, helplessly watching his teammates fight to keep the Hawks from shooting in a score.

But even Ed Courtney's fantastic moves couldn't stop them this time. It was Phil Adams again who swished the puck past him. The score was Phil's third, a hat trick. Hawks 4, Penguins 1.

Pie re-entered the game, eager to make up for lost time.

A Hawk got the pass on the face-off, passed it to a teammate, and Pie was after him as swiftly as his oversize shoeskates would allow. Just past the blue line, heading into Hawk territory, he jolted the Hawk with a neat bodycheck and stole the puck. Dribbling the black pellet with care, he swung around in a semicircle and started back across the blue line, then across the neutral zone into Penguin territory.

Two hawks charged after him and he flipped the puck to Bud. The puck rose

off the ice and flopped through the air between the two Hawks, bouncing in front
of Bud. Bud stopped it with his skate, then
snapped it back to Pie.

Pie, heading for the right-hand side of
the net, caught the puck and with one
sweeping motion shoved it hard toward
the narrow opening between the Hawk
goalie's padded leg and the goal.

Score!

"Nice shot, Pie!" Bud cried as the wingman skated up beside him.

"Thanks, Bud."

He looked for Terry and saw the center
sweeping around the net, totally ignoring
him.

The meathead, thought Pie. *I scored,
didn't I? He can't be mad at me for that!*

"All right, third line!" Coach Joe Hayes
yelled from the bench. "Off the ice!"

"I just get going and then I have to get off," Pie grunted as he headed for the sideline.

"That's your problem," said a voice at his elbow. "You always get started too late, if you ever get started at all."

Pie glanced over his shoulder at Terry. The blue eyes met his and held unflinchingly.

"Why do you keep riding me, Mason?" Pie asked. "What have I done to you?"

"Nothing to me! It's what you're doing to the team! I don't know about you, but I'd like to get on a winning team once in my life!"

So that was it, Pie thought. Terry was blaming him for the poor direction the team was going. *But why me?* he thought. *I'm not the only one who isn't playing like a big leaguer.*

He was sure there was something else bothering Terry. Something else that made the center pick on Pie more often than he did anyone else.

Line 2 failed to score. With fifty seconds to go in the game, Line 3 banged in a twenty-footer, and the game ended with the Hawks winning, 4 to 3.

The teams skated off the ice, the Hawks triumphantly loud over their victory, the Penguins quiet and cheerless. They had learned to accept losses without crying over them. There would be other games, other chances for victory.

But one man did feel differently about losing. Terry "the terrible" Mason, who slammed down his skates on the bench and sourly left the gym.

Pie was met with a surprise greeting at the gate. The twins! He quickly forgot about Terry.

"Got a minute?" Jody whispered.

Pie stepped toward the wall with them, out of the way of the people leaving the rink.

"Didn't think you guys were here," he said. "What is it?"

Both twins looked at him as if they had something on their minds that couldn't wait another minute.

"We played a game last night and it was exactly like this one, Pie!" Jody said excitedly. "Exactly!"

Pie stared.

"Even to my getting penalized?"

"Right! Even to that!" Joliette exclaimed.

6

PIE SAT down in the locker room to take off his skates and saw Coach Hayes and Terry Mason talking together near the far wall.

Terry looked at him, and something flashed in his eyes that made Pie suspect that it was he they were talking about.

He blushed and with nervous fingers began to unlace his shoeskates. What was Terry up to now?

A few minutes later Pie left the locker room. Outside, in the bright sunshine, Bud Rooney caught up with him.

"Bud," Pie said, "what were the coach and Terry talking about?"

"You," said Bud directly.

Pie's heart skipped a beat. "That's what I figured. Did you hear what they said?"

"Not all of it," Bud replied. "But I think Terry asked to play on another line."

"What did Coach say?"

"I don't know. He didn't talk as loud as Terry did."

So, Pie thought, *the great Terry "the terrible" Mason doesn't want to play on the same line with me anymore. Suits me fine. I don't exactly enjoy playing with him either. Not with him on my back all the time.*

He couldn't guess, though, just what the coach proposed to do. He would have to wait till the next game.

That afternoon he went over to the

twins' house and found them downstairs in the recreation room, busy as beavers, drawing pollution posters.

"Our class is conducting a contest," Joliette explained enthusiastically. "The best poster on pollution wins two free tickets to a movie."

SHOW YOU CARE BY CLEARING THE AIR, read the bold heading of her poster. Underneath she had started to sketch tall smokestacks of a factory.

KILLING FISH AT SEA IS THEIR CUP OF TEA was the title of Jody's poster. Jody was sketching a weird-looking monster holding a huge cup supposedly representing an ocean. On the surface of the cup were several fish lying flat on their side, presumably dead. POLLUTION was scrawled on the monster's headdress.

Pie's jaws slackened. He had come over with hopes of playing with their toy hockey game.

"I suppose you guys won't have time to play a game of hockey since you have those posters to work on," he said.

"Oh, yes, we have!" Joliette cried, dropping her pencil. "These don't have to be in till next Thursday!"

Pie looked at her, then at Jody. He hadn't particularly considered her as his opponent. He had considered Jody.

"Well, ah . . ." he stammered, embarrassed. "Only two can play the game at the same time. Why don't you work on your poster, Jolie, while Jody and I play?"

Surprisingly, she agreed. "Okay. I understand perfectly. I'm a girl and you prefer playing with a boy. It's perfectly logical — to a boy, I guess."

She took up her pencil again and continued to work on the poster, showing only the least bit of disappointment.

Pie laughed. "You can play the winner," he said.

He and Jody went over to the table where the hockey game was set up, selected their sides and started to play. An old clock on a shelf beside them served as a timer.

"Three periods, twelve minutes each," Pie said. "Just like a real game."

They started to play. Within three minutes Jody scored a goal. Pie tied it up, and the game continued with each scoring twice before the period was over.

"Have you picked out yourself in the game?" Jody asked.

"That right wingman," Pie pointed. "I think he's doing better than I could, though." He paused, then said seriously, "Jody, do you really think I'll be playing like he is at our game next Saturday?"

"No," Jody said. "I think this game works only when we play it the day before the real game. That's the way it's been working out anyway."

"Then playing now doesn't mean anything?"

"I don't think so. But I'm not really sure, Pie. We can only wait and see."

"Well, if it does, playing this game might help me," Pie said, thoughtfully. "If it doesn't, at least we've had a lot of fun."

"How can it help you?" Jody asked.

"I'm slow on the ice," Pie confessed, then chuckled. "Haven't you heard Terry Mason? He broadcasts it like a radio announcer."

"Yes, I heard him." Jody scowled. "He gives me a pain."

Pie shrugged. "He's right in a lot of ways, though. I am slow, but it's not all my fault. It's my shoeskates. They're too big. They used to belong to my brother, Pat."

He didn't mind confiding that information to Jody. Jody wouldn't tell a soul.

Suddenly he saw a movement from the corner of his left eye. He turned abruptly and looked at the window above the shelf where the clock stood. The curtains were partly drawn, letting in daylight.

A face was there, and a pair of large, inquisitive eyes was staring down at them.

7

QUICKLY THE face disappeared, but not before Pie had recognized it. He looked wide-eyed at Jody.

"Did you see who that was?"

"Yes. Terry Mason." Angrily Jody ran over to the curtains and snapped them shut. "Man, he's got nerve."

"Wonder if he heard us talking."

"Probably. Did you see that grin on his face? He seemed to be getting a kick out of what he heard."

They finished the game, Pie winning by two goals. He wasn't especially pleased to play with Joliette, but he had promised her that the winner would play her and he couldn't back out.

He beat her by one point.

"You're almost better than Jody," he said frankly.

She shrugged. "Even though we're twins," she said, "I firmly think that I'm inclined to be more athletic than he is."

"Oh, sure," Jody said.

Pie thanked them for letting him play and then left. He saw Terry outside, packing snowballs and throwing them at a tree. Clinging close to his feet was his faithful cat, Tipper.

"Hi, Pie," Terry greeted, grinning. "Quite a hockey game the twins have, isn't it?"

Pie frowned. How much did Terry hear, anyway?

"What do you mean?"

"Well, it's magic, isn't it? Each player on your team represents one of us on the Penguins. Right?"

Pie let a smile curve his lips. *The best way to handle Terry Mason,* he thought, *is to agree with him.* "If you say so," he said.

"How many goals did you score? I mean *you* — not the whole team."

"Two," Pie answered.

"And I?"

"Two."

Terry scooped up a handful of snow, packed it into a firm ball and pegged it at the tree again. *Smack!* Right in the middle of its trunk.

"And you think that game will be just like the game we're playing Saturday?"

"Not necessarily."

Terry looked at him. "I thought that's what you guys said."

"You stuck your nose close enough to the window, but not your ears," Pie declared. "We said *maybe* it'll be like the game Saturday. We're not sure."

"Oh."

Terry's ears reddened as Pie, a wide grin on his face, headed for home. Let the smarty-pants believe what he wants to. He'll probably get so confused he won't know whether or not to believe that the twins' hockey game is really magic.

During the rest of the week he wondered, too, if the real game on Saturday morning would turn out to be like the one he had played with Jody. It hardly seemed likely. The last two real games were like the ones the twins had played on their toy game the Friday nights before the actual matches. It would seem that the pattern would remain the same.

On Friday afternoon, just after he had arrived home from school, there was a knock on the door. Pie answered it. It was Jody Byrd, looking as excited as if he had just seen a flying saucer.

"Hi, Pie! Coming over for a game of hockey?"

Pie considered. "I don't think I will, Jody," he confessed. "It might be like our game tomorrow, and I don't think I'd like to know beforehand how it goes. You know."

"Oh, okay. Anyway, Jolie and I have our posters done, and we made a discovery."

Pie's eyebrows arched. "What discovery?"

"We figured out what S-K-X-R-O-T

really is," Jody said proudly. "Remember Merlin the magician in the story of King Arthur?"

Pie's forehead knitted. "Yes."

"Well, in the alphabet, six letters to the right of each letter in Merlin's name spells S-K-X-R-O-T!"

Pie stared. "How'd you discover that?"

"By experimenting," Jody explained. "Jolie helped me, of course. We figured it must be a code, so we wrote the alphabet on two separate sheets of paper, then put one under the other, passing it along underneath each letter to see if S-K-X-R-O-T would spell out a word we were familiar with. Sure enough it came up with Merlin. And both of us have read about him in the King Arthur books."

"Then Merlin the magician must've been a real person," said Pie, feeling goosebumps on his arms.

"Must've," said Jody. "Well, see you tomorrow, Pie."

Jody left, and Pie was in the act of closing the door when he spotted a familiar figure across the street. *Terry Mason,* he thought, *seems to be around a lot lately when you least expect him.*

And Pie saw as he looked harder that the confused look was still on Terry's face, too.

He smiled as he closed the door.

The game at 9:00 on Saturday morning was against the Seals, a team wearing blue uniforms with white trim. As he skated around the ice to warm up for the game, Pie looked at the stands for the familiar faces of the twins. He saw them finally, waved, and they waved back.

Wonder how their game turned out? he thought. *And I wonder how I played?*

He pushed the thoughts out of his mind

as a skater whisked past him, spun half way around and skated backward, facing him. Their eyes met and held. This time not even a flicker of a smile spoiled the wax-like features of Terry's face.

Near the corner of the rink Terry spun half way around again and continued skating frontward. *He's baffled,* Pie thought. *He doesn't believe in magic, so he doesn't know what to think about me, the twins, or their toy hockey game.*

Now that I've got him guessing maybe he'll lay off me, Pie thought. *But I'd better not count on it.*

Face-off time rolled around, and the first lines of both teams got in position on the ice. Terry centered against Corky Jones, a boy shorter than Terry, but muscular and fast.

The whistle shrilled, the puck was dropped, and the centers' sticks clattered

78

against the ice for possession of the puck. The rubber disk took a severe battering, then skittered across the ice into Penguin territory. Bud Rooney hooked it with the blade of his stick, whisked around, and started back up the ice. Pie, moving slowly in the neutral zone toward his own blue line, waited for the puck to cross into Seal territory.

Challenged by a Seal who came upon him suddenly from behind, Bud snapped the puck. Pie sprinted across the blue line in an effort to get in front of it, and *shreek!* the whistle pulled him up short.

"You were off side, Pennelli!" Terry yelled.

Pie blushed. That was stupid, he admitted. He had misjudged the speed of the puck and had caused a violation by crossing the blue line before the puck had.

The face-off was at the Penguin end of the rink between Frog and a Seal wingman. The Seal got control of the puck, passed it to another Seal, who caught it and bolted for the Penguin net. Pie lunged forward, sprinting as hard as he could to get between the goal and the oncoming Seal.

Suddenly his left skate twisted and his ankle gave way, throwing him off balance. He fell, skidded on the ice, and a player in a black uniform toppled over him.

A storming "You idiot!" identified the skater. It was Terry.

Terry clambered to his feet, his eyes blazing hot. Behind him a cry of jubilation had exploded, and Pie could see sticks rising in the air like spears as the Seals celebrated their first goal.

"I'm sorry," Pie apologized. "My ankle gave way."

"Your ankle!" Terry scoffed. "You know what's the matter with you? You haven't learned how to keep your balance yet, and you're trying to cut corners going eighty miles an hour! Well, you can't do that, Pie! You have to learn to keep your balance first!"

"C'mon, you guys!" yelled Coach Hayes. "Off the ice!"

Line 1 skated off and Line 2 skated on. Pie, tired and sweaty, avoided the coach's eyes as he climbed over the wall and sat down. *Terry had no business talking to me like that,* he thought. *Not on the ice in front of all that crowd. Not anywhere.*

One of these days I'm going to surprise him, Pie promised himself. I'll break every one of his teeth.

The fault was in his shoeskates, of course. *But if I told that to Terry,* Pie thought, *he'd laugh and say that that ex-*

cuse was worse than none.

He watched Line 2 and then Line 3 do their stuff, and helped in the cheering when Butch Morrison, Line 3's center for the Penguins, knocked in a goal to knot the score.

Back on the ice went Line 1, and this time Pie tried his best not to cut corners sharply and risk a spill. But after awhile he realized that he might as well have stayed off the ice as stick rigidly to that rule. Playing hockey *was* skating as fast as you could, stopping quickly as you could, and cutting corners as sharply as possible. There was no other way to play the game and play it well. Fall or not, that was the way he was going to play it.

Terry, he told himself, could lump it.

An offside violation was called on Chuck Billings. And on the face-off in neutral territory Bud got the pass and shot it to Terry. Terry dribbled the puck up the ice, across the blue line and into Seals' territory. He was suddenly trapped by two Seals who came swooping down at him from different directions.

He tried to pass the puck between them to Bud Rooney, but one of the Seals stopped it with his skate. The puck skidded to the side and Pie, speeding down the ice near the boards, cut in and snared it. Pulling the puck safely toward him, he put on a burst of speed and carried it down the ice toward the Seals' goal.

From ten feet away he shot.

A save!

"Why didn't you pass it, Pie?" Bud Rooney cried.

There, on the other side of the crease,

Pie saw the wingman in the open.

Pie skated around the back of the net, coming up behind Bud. "Sorry, Bud," he said.

"Sure," Bud grumbled.

"Come on, you guys! Move! Move!" yelled Coach Hayes.

Too late both Pie and Bud saw the fast breakaway the Seals had made. Two of them had the puck up the ice, and the only Penguin on their tails was Terry Mason.

A quick pass to the wingman on the left, then a pass back to the wingman on the right. Then — *snap!*

Goal!

Pie slowed down as he reached the net, and as the center made a sharp turn in front of the crease and skated up to him, Pie found himself face to face with Terry.

"If you want to rest why don't you get off the ice?" Terry growled. "Those guys had the puck halfway up the ice while you were still yakking with Bud."

"I just told him that I was sorry I didn't pass to him," said Pie. "What's wrong with that?"

Thirty seconds later a Seal stole the puck from Pie, sped alone down the ice, and belted it past Ed Courtney's left shoulder for a goal.

Pie looked on, stunned.

8

O FF THE ICE!" yelled the coach. "Pronto!"

Pie sprinted off, pulled up sharply near the boards, and stepped over the wall. As the other members of Line 1 skated off the ice, Line 2 scrambled on.

"That Seal surprise you, Pie?" Coach Hayes asked, smiling.

Pie, his chest heaving with each inhaled breath, nodded. He expected a lecture from the coach about the play, but Coach Hayes said nothing more.

There was nothing to say, anyway, Pie

thought. *The Seal just stole that puck from me and took off. That's all there was to it. The guy was just lucky he had open ice ahead of him. A thing like that doesn't happen often.*

And it's a good thing it doesn't, Pie thought grimly.

The teams' third lines scrambled onto the ice and then off again without scoring.

"Let's have some teamwork this period," Coach Hayes prompted as Line 1 got on the ice to start off the second period. "Terry, quit yelling at Pie out there or you might be watching the rest of the game from the bench."

"Who's yelling at him?" Terry snorted and zipped onto the ice without waiting for a reply.

The men skated to their positions. The face-off. The fight to control the puck.

Bang! Terry socked it to Bud. Bud dribbled it into Seal territory and was suddenly bodychecked, but not before he drove the puck against the boards. It bounced back onto the ice and skittered toward the Seals' goal where Pie and the two Seals' defensemen charged after it. Pie, feeling his oversize shoeskates hampering his speed, kicked the ice accidentally with the toe of his skate and fell flat on his stomach.

The Seals got the puck, passed it back up the ice and shot it to a wingman. Pie felt a hand grab his arm and help him to his feet.

He didn't see who his benefactor was until the guy had sped away on his skates. It was Terry.

Pie bolted after him, ignoring the powdery ice that covered the entire front of his uniform. He sped alongside the boards, this time trying not to stumble. It would be awful if Terry had to pick him up again.

Frog Alexander stole the puck away from a Seal and belted it up the ice to Terry. Terry swerved in a half circle, the puck hooked in the curve of the blade of his stick, and started back up the ice with it. Two Seals charged after him from his left and right sides, and he passed to Pie.

Pie stickhandled the puck across the blue line, then across the neutral zone into Seal territory. Now the Seals' defensemen were after him, arms and legs churning as they swept upon him like vultures. Far ahead he saw the Seals' goalie crouched in front of the net, wide open spaces around him.

Pie glanced at the puck — taking just enough time to make certain that the blade of his stick would strike it exactly right — and swung.

Smack! The puck lifted off the ice and sailed through the air like a miniature flying saucer. It headed for the upper right-hand corner of the net, just over the goalie's left shoulder. The goalie reached for it, and for a second his huge glove obscured the flying missile. It looked as if he had caught the puck, and Pie's heart sank.

Then he heard the exploding yell from the fans, and saw the goalie's arm dropping, and there in the corner of the net was the black disk falling to the ice.

"Nice shot, Pie!" Bud yelled, slapping him on the shoulder.

From the bench came the resounding thunder of Penguin sticks banging against the boards.

"All right, Line 1!" Coach Hayes

shouted. "Off the ice! Line 2, take over! *Do* something!"

Pie took his time skating off. His legs ached. His body was hot and sweaty. *I could go for a shower right now,* he thought.

"Nice shooting, Pie," Coach Hayes praised him as he stepped through the gate and sat down. "It was perfect."

He looked at the scoreboard. HOME 3, VISITORS 2. The VISITORS were the Penguins.

Line 2 held the Seals. Then Line 3 scored, tieing it up.

It was still 3 to 3 when the second period ended.

As Pie waited for the whistle that would signal the first lines to get back on the ice for the start of the third period, someone touched him on the shoulder.

"Pie!" a voice whispered into his ear.

He looked around. It was Jody Byrd, looking wide-eyed as ever.

"Yeah, what?" Pie asked.

Jody hesitated. "I don't know whether I should tell you this," he said reluctantly.

"Tell me what?" asked Pie.

"This last period is going to be bad," Jody replied. "Real bad."

Pie looked him straight in the eyes. "I'm sorry you told me," he said.

9

THE WHISTLE blew for the start of the third period, and Pie went onto the ice, his knees feeling like rubber.

He skated to his position opposite the Seals' wing and carefully watched the puck as the referee dropped it and the centers fought for its control. The pellet shot on edge toward the left side of the rink where both Bud Rooney and a Seals' defenseman pounced on it with their sticks.

Then the Seal whacked it against the boards. Pie, quickly determining where he might intercept the puck, sprinted to the spot as the rubber pellet bounced back. He hooked it with the blade of his stick and charged up the ice, skating parallel with the boards, stickhandling the puck with perfect ease. But his legs felt weak, and he knew he wasn't skating as fast as he normally could.

A Seal defenseman bolted up behind him and whisked the puck away from him before he realized what happened. Back up the ice the Seal swept the puck in the opposite direction. Pie watched, half stunned.

"C'mon, Pie!" Terry yelled. "Look alive!"

Pie pulled himself together and sprinted after the puck. He saw the Seal pass to a wingman who had swept in from the left side of the net. A quick snap sent the puck flying past Ed Courtney before the goalie could lift his arm. A goal!

Pie, head bowed, slowed down, turned, and coasted toward his position. He was bone-tired, and he dreaded the thought that he had to come onto the ice once again after this session.

"C'mon, Pie. Wake up," Terry said as he skated up beside the weary wingman. "If you're tired, why don't you get off the ice? Let somebody else take over."

Pie wanted to do that desperately, but he wouldn't go voluntarily. He preferred to have the coach call him off. It wouldn't look so bad if Coach Hayes yanked him.

The whistle shrilled, sending a shock wave through his head that made him squinch.

The face-off. Suddenly he saw the puck

skittering past his left skate. He caught it with his stick and carried it swiftly across the blue line and then the red line into Seal territory. A Seal charged at him. He saw no one to pass to, so he shot the puck against the boards. Then he bolted forward to catch the rebound. But a Seal defenseman reached it first and belted it across the ice to a wingman. Two passes and the puck was down near the Penguin goal. Ed Courtney was protecting the net with all the ability and agility he had, but he didn't have enough of either one.

The puck sailed past his padded left leg for the Seals' fifth goal.

The first lines went off the ice, replaced by the second lines, and Pie sat on the bench, his chest heaving.

"You're bushed, Pie," the coach said. "Didn't you get enough rest last night?"

Pie shrugged. He didn't answer.

The Penguins' second line had control of the puck during most of the time they were on the ice, but the Seals' goaltender matched every shot made at the net. He had five saves before the lines skated off the ice and the third lines skated on.

At 6:23 Butch Morrison, the Penguins' center for Line 3, scored, bringing them up within a goal of the leading Seals, 5 to 4.

Terry looked at Pie as they skated toward their positions.

"I suppose you're playing this last time because of that toy hockey game," Terry said.

Pie glanced at him. "What do you mean by that?"

Terry's lips curved in a half smile. "You know what I mean. That toy hockey game the Byrd twins found in their attic is supposed to be magic, isn't it?"

"Oh." Pie shrugged. "Yeah. I suppose it is. Real genuine magic."

They skated past the center spot and were heading for the right forward position, yet Terry had made no attempt to stop.

"So now you're sure you know our secret," Pie said, stopping at his position. Terry remained silent, and Pie knew that the center was only guessing. Terry really wasn't sure whether or not to believe Pie about the toy hockey game's being endowed with magical powers.

The whistle shrilled. "C'mon, Terry," the ref snapped. "Let's go."

Terry shot Pie a final questioning look, then skated to his position at center. A trace of a smile flickered over Pie's face.

The ref dropped the puck, and the clock started up again for Line 1's last time on the ice. *Maybe Terry was still thinking of the toy hockey game,* Pie thought, *because Corky Jones, the Seals' center, got the drop on him.* He slapped the puck away, sprinted after it himself, then shot it to a wingman heading up the ice alongside the boards.

Pie bolted down the rink on the opposite side, staying in the clear in case either Bud or Frog managed to intercept the puck. Near the corner Frog bodychecked the speeding Seal wingman, who passed the puck to a teammate sprinting up center ice toward the Penguins' goal.

Slap! A beautiful drive directly at the net! Ed Courtney got in front of it and stopped it expertly with his padded chest. A save. The puck dropped in front of him, and he covered it with his glove.

The whistle blew. Calmly, Ed picked up the puck and tossed it to the ref.

Again the face-off, and the black pellet

skittered to Pie. He pushed it gently ahead of him, heading toward the right corner of the Seals' net.

At the back of his mind echoed Jody Byrd's whispered warning. *This last period is going to be bad. Real bad.*

How bad could it be? Pie wondered.

Suddenly blue and white uniforms converged on him, with sticks looking like the tentacles of a ruffled octopus. Pie glanced quickly behind and saw both Bud and Terry approaching from the other side of the net, waiting for him to pass.

He struck the puck. It hit the skate of one of the Seals and bounced back, and he found himself scrambling for it with the two Seals. His face was hot and his arms and legs felt like iron weights.

Suddenly his vision got hazy. His head

swam, and his legs became like jelly. Someone collided into him and down he went, hitting the ice hard. He lay there in a sea of blackness, while far away a whistle shrilled in short, sharp blasts.

He was tired and sleepy. So tired and sleepy.

After a while his head cleared. His vision became normal, and he heard Coach Hayes' voice. "Feel better, Pie? Can you get up?"

He nodded, and the coach helped him to his feet and off the ice.

It wasn't until he was sitting on the bench that he noticed a Seal sitting in the penalty box across the rink.

"What's he in for?" Pie asked.

"Illegal bodychecking," Coach Hayes said.

"On me?"

"Yes."

Pie frowned. "But it wasn't his fault. It was mine. I've been bushed. Real bushed. I — I just passed out, that's all."

"That's what I thought, too," Coach Hayes said. "I shouldn't have let you go out there this last time."

He watched the rest of the game from the bench. There was no more scoring, and the Seals won, 5 to 4.

The Byrd twins met Pie outside and walked home with him. Pie noticed that Terry was trailing behind them, trying to get within earshot of what they were saying. He warned them not to say anything about the toy hockey game until Terry was gone.

"Well, did the game come out like the toy game did?" he asked, when Terry was no longer trailing.

105

"It sure did," Jody said. "Except that we didn't know what happened to you in our game. Our hockey players don't get knocked down, you know!"

Pie laughed. "How did that part show up in your game?"

"Simple. You and two Seals kept scrambling for the puck. Suddenly you stopped moving."

"I did?"

"Yes. Just long enough for Jolie — I mean one of the Seals — to grab the puck and pass it on."

"But why did I stop moving? Or how?" Pie wanted to know, staring wide-eyed from one twin to the other.

Jody shrugged. "You just jammed, that's all. You didn't move." His cheeks dimpled. "I suppose that's when you were knocked out!"

Pie grinned. "I suppose," he said.

He saw the twins off and on during the next few days. But it wasn't until Friday that Jody called and told him some shocking news.

"Something's happened to our hockey game, Pie! Jolie and I looked high and low for it, but we can't find it anywhere!"

Pie frowned. "You have no idea what's happened to it?" he asked.

"No! We just know it's missing!"

10

PIE WENT over to the twins' house to help look for the game. Immediately he noticed a difference in the basement from the last time he had visited it. The tiled floor was polished and the furniture dusted. Something else seemed different about it, but he couldn't quite figure out what it was.

"Has the furniture been changed around?" he asked the twins. "Something looks different."

"Dad moved the sofa from that wall to that one," Joliette explained, pointing to a paneled wall and then to the sofa underneath the basement window.

A look at the window drew a double-take from Pie.

"I don't remember seeing that window open before," he said.

"Dad must've opened it when he cleaned here last night," Jody said. "He does that to air the basement out."

"No one could've come in through there, if that's what you're thinking," said Joliette. "There's a screen behind it. Anyway, who would do a thing like that?"

"Terry 'the terrible' Mason, maybe?" Jody said, his eyebrows arching as he glanced at Pie.

Pie shrugged. "Well, we saw him peeking in that window. He knows where you kept the game."

He looked at the table at the far side

of the room on which the twins had kept the game always ready for play. The regular four chairs were grouped around it.

"Are you sure your father didn't put it somewhere?"

"Why should he?" Jody said. "He knows that Jolie and I play with it a lot."

"Have you asked him?"

"He isn't home. He won't be till tomorrow afternoon," replied Jody.

"He's a salesman," Joliette explained.

"I suppose you've asked your mother about it?"

"Of course," Joliette replied. "But she doesn't know a thing about it."

Pie sighed. "I wonder how that'll affect tomorrow's game."

"Why should it?" Joliette asked.

"It always did before," said Pie. A thought occurred to him. "I wonder what would happen if Terry had taken it," he said. "Up till now he isn't sure whether it has magical powers or not. He's just been guessing. Maybe he wants to experiment with it."

"Think it'll work for him?" Jody said.

"Why not? It's magic. The power is in the game, isn't it? Not in the people who play it."

He went out and paused on the curb of the sun-drenched street. There, beside the tree where Pie had seen him once before, stood Terry Mason. Smiling. At his feet was his favorite companion, Tipper.

Pie braced himself.

"Terry," he said, "have you got the twins' hockey game?"

Terry stared at him. "The twins' hockey game?" he echoed. The smile vanished. "What would I want with their old hockey game?"

"It's missing," Pie said.

Terry's fists clenched as he came at Pie. "Are you accusing me of stealing it, Pie-face?"

Pie stood his ground. "We saw you looking through the window the other night," he said defiantly.

"That doesn't mean I stole it!" Terry snapped. "Maybe it disappeared by itself. It *was* magic, wasn't it?" A laugh of mockery tore from his lips.

Pie matched his glaring eyes, not certain whether to believe him or not. "See you at the rink," he said.

He felt a rubbing against his leg, looked down and saw Tipper looking up at him, eyes like large yellow marbles.

"Hi, Tipper," Pie said, smiling.

"*Meow!*" Tipper said.

Terry picked it up. "C'mon, Tip," he said, walking away, "before he starts ask-

ing *you* questions about that dumb hockey game."

Pie lay in bed that night thinking about the missing game. What could have happened to it, anyway? Had someone really stolen it from the basement, or had Mr. Byrd put it somewhere where the twins were unable to find it? Or, as Terry had suggested, had it disappeared? Did the game really possess such magical powers that it *could* disappear by itself?

It was a long time before sleep finally overtook him.

The next morning, as he was putting on his uniform to prepare for the game against the Bears, he heard the distant ring of the telephone and a few moments later his mother's voice, "Pie! Never mind getting dressed!"

He froze and stared at the door. Then

he went to it and shouted down the hall, "Mom! What did you say?"

"Coach Hayes just called," she said from the bottom of the stairs. "He said that the game's called off."

He stared, shivers rippling up his spine. "Did he say why, Mom?"

"The electric power's off," she explained. "The game is postponed till some future date."

11

AFTER BREAKFAST Pie went over to the Byrds' house and told the twins the sad news. Their eyes popped. Their mouths sagged open.

"Isn't that something?" Jody whispered tensely.

"That toy hockey game has more magical powers than I realized!" Joliette exclaimed in the same breathless whisper. "It's fantastic!"

"Fantastic is right," replied Pie, keeping his voice down too so as not to let Mrs. Byrd hear. No telling what she might say if she heard them discussing magical powers. "I've talked with Terry Mason about it. I practically accused him of stealing the game."

"What did he say?" Joliette asked.

"He said he didn't steal it. And was he mad!"

"Do you think he did?" Jody inquired.

"I don't think so. He wouldn't have gotten so sore if he had. I was sorry afterwards that I accused him. It was a dumb thing to do, since I was only guessing, anyway."

"Yeah, that's right," said Jody. "Well, it's going to be a dull day now that the hockey game was called off. Wonder what will happen if we never find our hockey game?"

"Good question," said Pie.

Joliette shivered. "We've got to find it,"

she said. "I won't ever sleep again if we don't."

It wasn't a dull day for Pie. His father started to build a partition in the basement to make a carpenter shop for himself, and Pie helped him. Working got his mind off the missing toy hockey game. But when they finished for the day his thoughts reverted back to it.

What effect would there be on the real hockey rink if the toy hockey game could never be found again?

It was something to worry about.

At five minutes of eight that night Jody called. His voice was bubbling with excitement.

"We've found the hockey game, Pie!" he cried.

Pie's heart skipped a beat. "Where was it?"

"Dad had put it on a shelf in the basement and then covered it with an old rug! Unintentionally!"

A wave of relief swept over Pie. "That's the best news I've heard in years, Jody," he said. "Well, there's something I must do now, for sure."

"What?" Jody asked.

"Apologize to Terry," Pie replied. "And I can think of a million things I'd rather do than that!"

"I know what you mean," Jody said. "But I suppose it's best. It'll rest on your conscience if you don't."

"Right," said Pie. "Well, thanks for the good news, Jody. See you."

"How about coming over next Friday night and playing a game?"

"Okay! See you then."

It was after church on Sunday morning

when Pie met Terry and considered apologizing to him. But their parents were around, and Pie couldn't gather up enough nerve.

Later that day, when he was returning from the gorge after a look at the ice-caked falls, he met Terry again. Terry had his cat with him, trailing at his heels.

"Terry, I — I want to see you a minute," Pie said. His heart was thumping. He'd rather jump into ice-cold water than apologize to Terry Mason. But, as Jody Byrd had said, the guilt would rest on his conscience if he didn't.

"That's a switch," Terry said.

"I owe you an apology," Pie said. "I accused you of stealing that hockey game from the Byrd twins, and I'm sorry."

"Why? Did they find it?"

"Yes. Mr. Byrd had stuck it up on a

121

shelf, then covered it with an old rug." The thumping began to disappear. "Well, that's all I wanted to say."

Terry looked at him a long minute. "Okay," he said at last.

They passed by each other and continued on their way. Suddenly Terry yelled, "Pie?"

Pie looked around. "Yes?"

Terry was holding his cat. "Thanks!"

"Sure," said Pie.

There was an item in the *Deep Gorge News* Monday evening about the electric power system's being repaired at Davis Rink and that the game between the Penguins and the Hawks would be played as scheduled. The Penguins–Bears game, which was called off last Saturday morning due to the power's being off, would be played sometime in January

On Friday night Pie went over to the

twins' house again. After visiting for a while with Mr. and Mrs. Byrd, he and the twins descended to the basement, sat at the table in front of the toy hockey game, chose their teams and started to play. Since tomorrow's game was with the Hawks, Jody called his team the Hawks and Pie called his the Penguins. Joliette kept time and the score.

The game started with the usual face-off at center. Jody's man grabbed the puck, zipped down the rink and *swish!* A shot that missed the goal by a hair.

The puck bounced off the corner and into the rink, and Pie raced after it with a defensive player. The player brought the puck up the ice, shot it across the blue line, and a Penguin wingman stopped it.

"That's you, Pie!" Joliette cried excitedly.

So it was, Pie realized. He moved the

man up the ice, and *snap!* The man spun and the puck shot off the edge of his stick. Missed!

The puck whipped around the corner. Jody's man intercepted it, shot, and again Pie caught it.

Slap! A close one! But again a miss.

One of Jody's men grabbed the puck, carried it up the ice and shot. Goal!

"Sorry about that," Jody said, grinning.

In the second period Pie tried his best to tie up the score, but his shots kept missing by slim margins. Then he tried a new tack. He passed to another player, not realizing who it was until the player scored and Joliette shouted, "That man's Terry, Pie!"

The fast action continued, and Pie found himself sweating. He blamed it on the excitement and the action, but he knew that the real reason for it was knowing that the game was a preview of tomorrow's real game.

Almost halfway through the second period the man who represented him passed to the man representing Terry, and again the man scored.

"You're ahead, Pie!" Joliette shouted.

Pie smiled. Perhaps that was the smart thing to do — keep passing to Terry, regardless of how they felt toward each other. Playing the best together was the way to play the game.

Then, about a minute later, Pie's right wing failed to budge when Pie twisted the control lever. He twisted it this way and that, but the figure remained almost stationary.

That's me again, he realized, staring. *Would that mean disaster in the real game?* A chill ran down his spine.

12

"TIME!" PIE called, and Joliette wrote down the time on a notepad.

Pie tried to lift the hockey figure off the metal rod that projected straight up out of the slot about an inch, and it slid off easily.

"It's gotten loose," Jody observed.

"Twisting it so many times must've loosened it," Pie reasoned. "Those little staples in the wood came out just enough to lose their hold on the rod."

There were two such staples driven into the hockey figure, square ones to fit over the square rods. He put the hockey figure back in place, fitted the staples over the rod, then tried to force the staples further into the wood with his thumb. He couldn't.

"Get me something to tap them with," he said.

Jody produced a hammer from a wall laden with tools and handed it to him. A light tap on each staple made the hockey figure secure again. Pie twisted the controls back and forth, and the figure whipped this way and that like new.

"Well, I'm in shape again," he said happily. "But it's funny why that happened to *me*. The man representing me, I mean."

"I thought of that," said Jody. "Think it really means something, Pie?"

"I don't know. I won't know till we play tomorrow."

"In my opinion it definitely means

something," Joliette said with conviction. "I don't know what and I don't think it's serious, because you're back in the game. But I bet it means *something*."

"But those staples coming loose could be just an accident," Pie said.

"No accident," Jody said, as he jiggled the other figures on their rods. "Look. Every one of them is tight. Why should the staples only on yours come loose?"

Pie inhaled deeply and emptied his lungs with a long, drawn-out sigh. "That's right," he said. "Why?"

"Let's finish the game," Jody suggested. "Let's see what else is going to happen tomorrow."

"You two finish it," Pie said, feeling a tension mounting inside him. "I don't think I'd care to know what else is going to happen to me tomorrow."

He left the table.

"Maybe that's what it meant!" Joliette cried. "You'll be leaving the game!"

"For good?" Her brother wrinkled his nose. "Nuts, Jolie. That's only the second period. What *might* happen is that Pie will go out for a while for some reason *other* than a normal one, and then go back in again."

"You could've let me finish," Joliette said, glaring at him.

"Sorry. Sure you don't want to finish the game, Pie?"

"I'm sure," said Pie. "See you tomorrow — after the game."

The rest of the evening — from the time he left the twins till he went to bed — dragged like a snail crossing the Mojave Desert. So did the morning — from the time he got up till the time he went to the

131

game. What *did* that accident in the toy hockey game mean, anyway?

The buzzer sounded for the start of the game and the Line 1 players of both the Hawks and the Penguins skated to their positions. The whistle shrilled.

Face-off!

Phil Adams, the Hawks' center, knocked the puck to his left wingman. The man scooted down the length of the ice close to the boards, then cut in sharply toward the Penguins' net. Just as Frog Alexander swooped toward him, his stick outstretched to pokecheck the puck, the Hawk shot. Like a missile the black pellet flew through the air toward the net — and missed by inches!

The puck bounced off the wall behind the net, Pie after it. The defensive Hawk beside him reached the puck first, and

Pie bumped into him. He tried to hold his balance as he scrambled to pokecheck the puck, but his oversize shoeskates prevented him from shifting around as quickly as he wanted to. In a second he found himself sprawled on the ice while the Hawk defenseman dribbled the puck toward Penguin territory.

"Come on, Pie!" yelled a familiar voice. "On your feet!"

He scrambled up, ignoring Terry Mason's commanding yell. Apparently apologizing to Terry for accusing him of stealing the Byrd twins' toy hockey game hadn't changed his attitude a bit.

Pie saw the Hawk defenseman glancing at a wing, and sprinted up the ice. Just as Frog and Terry met the oncoming Hawk, the man snapped a pass to the wing.

Anticipating the play, Pie bolted forward, stretched out his stick, and intercepted the pass. He sprinted for the net. Ten feet from it he shot. The puck sailed through the air. Up went the Hawk goalie's hand. A save!

A minute later Pie accepted a pass from Frog, shot, and again the Hawk goalie's gloved hand picked it out of the air like a frog's quick tongue catching a fly.

Oh, man! Pie thought disappointedly. *I can't get one through him!*

The face-off. Then a Hawk was dribbling the puck up the ice, stickhandling it as if the pellet was magnetized to his stick. My man! Pie realized, and sprinted after him.

The Hawk swept by Frog, weaved around Chuck and reached the side of the Penguins' net. *Snap!* There were only inches between Ed Courtney's padded legs and the side of the net, but the puck sailed through for a Hawks' score.

"That was your man, Pie!" Terry snapped as the first line skated off the ice and the second line skated on.

"I can see," Pie replied indignantly. "But these skates are — "

He caught himself and met Terry's flashing eyes.

"Skates are what?" Terry asked, smiling. "Too small? Too big? I was wondering when you were going to blame *something.*"

"Fact is, they are big," Pie said as they climbed over the wall and sat down. "They belonged to my brother. And his feet are bigger than mine. Lots bigger."

Terry's lips parted as if he were going

to say something, then closed again. The reaction surprised Pie. It wasn't like Terry to shut up like a clam. *Something that I said*, Pie thought, *had made him change his mind.*

What?

Pie remembered that Bob, Terry's older brother and a former hockey player here at Deep Gorge, was also attending State College. "What do you hear from Bob?" he asked, hoping that a little dialogue might help Terry forget his differences with him.

"Nothing," Terry said.

"He's playing, isn't he?"

"Yeah. Yeah, sure."

He didn't seem to want to talk any more about Bob, and Pie didn't push him. But it sure was funny how he had clammed up so fast.

The score remained 1 to 0 going into the second period. Line 1 was back on the ice. This is the period, Pie thought — a shiver racing up his spine — when something is supposed to happen to me.

But after a few moments on the ice he forgot the incident, forgot last night, forgot everything except what was happening now.

Twice he took shots at the goal and missed. Each time he expected a yell from Terry, but the center was keeping silent. Pie couldn't believe it. Had mentioning Pat's skates to him really made that much difference?

A Hawk was dribbling the puck past Pie. Pie sped after him, bodychecked him near the defensive blue line, grabbed the puck and bolted up the ice with it. Ten feet from the Hawks' net he met the oncoming Hawk defensemen and considered taking a shot. Suddenly he saw one of his own men skating in from the left side of the net. It was Terry. Instinctively, Pie shot the puck to him. Terry caught it, and *snap!* Into the net for a goal!

Terry glided by Pie, and was instantly smothered by the other Penguins. "Nice going, Terry!" "Great shot, man!" they shouted.

Pie skated around the net, a spark of pride kindled in his heart. Terry was getting the praises, but it was Pie who had passed him the puck. And an assist, like a score, counted as a point, too.

The clock was ticking off the seconds toward the ten-minute mark when Pie intercepted a Hawk rebound off the boards and sprinted down center ice with it. As Pie breezed over the blue line into Hawk territory, a Hawk rammed into him with a neat bodycheck and knocked him down. The Hawk wingman quickly stretched out his stick, hooked its blade around the puck, and yanked it toward him.

Scrambling to his feet, Pie maneuvered himself between the Hawk and the puck, then shifted quickly and sped around the Hawk toward the opponents' net. The rink was open in front of him, and he was about to swat the puck for a shot at the goal, when both the goalie and a Hawk defenseman got in the line of fire.

Just then Pie saw a Penguin sweeping in from the left. It was Terry. Pie snapped the puck to him. The pass was perfect. Terry stopped it, and with a quick snap, scored.

Again Terry received the plaudits from his teammates. This time he skated up to

Pie, puffing hard. "Thanks, Pie," he said. "And also for the first one."

Pie, dead tired, only smiled.

"Nice passwork, Pie," Coach Hayes said to him as Line 1 came off the ice and Line 2 went on. "By the way, I heard you asking Terry about his brother, Bob."

"Yes."

"Did you know that Bob didn't make the team?"

Pie stared. "No, I didn't."

"Of course Pat did and is doing real well," said the coach. "Come to think of it, Pie, maybe that's why Terry's been bugging you. He's hurt that Bob isn't playing and Pat is, and has been taking it out on you."

Like a bombshell Pie realized the logic of that reasoning. Terry was a kid who would do exactly that.

"That must be it, Coach," he said. "It can't be anything else."

Line 2 couldn't score, but they held the Hawks from scoring, too. Line 3 did well until 6:23, when a Hawk drove in a shot to tie up the score, 2 to 2.

Meanwhile, Pie rested and tried to remember what had happened in the game he had played with Jody Byrd last night. But he was so tired he gave up.

Coach Hayes' yell, "Okay, Line 1, on the ice!" came ever too quickly.

The Hawks grabbed the puck from face-off and worked it toward the Penguins' goal with expert stickhandling before Frog managed to steal it and drive it back up the ice. Just before it reached the blue line, and to prevent an icing charge, Pie snared it. He started to dribble it through the neutral zone into

Hawk territory when a man bumped into him with a hard bodycheck and sent him sprawling.

Pie clambered to his feet and a sudden discovery reeled him. Something was wrong with his right skate!

He looked and his heart sank.

The front part of the skate had broken loose from the shoe!

13

PIE LEFT the ice, bone-tired and sick at heart. He'd have to watch the rest of the game from the bench, but what about afterward? Was he finished with skating? Would his father buy him a new pair?

The coach sent Jim Stanton in to replace him. Jim was a wing on Line 2.

"Too bad, Pie," Coach Hayes said. "But those skates looked too big for you in the first place. Were they?"

Pie nodded.

"Thought so. Skates should fit tighter than your regular shoes," Coach Hayes advised. "When you get your new pair, make sure they're a tight fit." He grinned and squeezed Pie's knee. "You'll find that you'll skate a lot better."

Seconds later someone tapped him on the shoulder. He looked around. It was Jody.

"That's what that trouble meant!" Jody whispered.

Pie frowned. "What trouble?"

Suddenly he knew what Jody was referring to. The hockey figure representing him on the toy hockey game coming loose on the rod last night! It had forecast today's incident as closely as anything possibly could!

"That's right!" Pie said breathlessly. "That's really right! And it happened in the second period, too! Just like it did here!"

Just then laughter exploded from the fans, and a whistle shrilled.

"Hey, look!" Jody shouted, pointing.

Pie looked, and there on the ice — running and slipping and sliding on its haunches near the Hawks' goal — was a calico cat!

"It's Tipper! Terry's cat!"

"Tipper!" Terry shouted and skated after it. He scooped it up and carried it gingerly to a little, blond-haired girl behind the boards. The girl, Pie saw, was Terry's sister, Pam.

The laughter changed to applause as Pam sat down with the cat on her lap, and Terry returned to the ice, shaking his head and smiling.

The game resumed. Seconds before Line 1 left the ice Terry knocked in his third score of the game with an assist by

Jim Stanton, the kid who had replaced Pie.

"A hat trick!" Pie cried, applauding. "Nice shot, Terry! Nice pass, Jim!"

"Thought you didn't like him," Jody said from behind him.

Pie shrugged. "Oh, he's really not as terrible as he pretends to be."

The game went into the third period, and finally ended, 3 to 2, in the Penguins' favor. Terry Mason had scored every goal for the Penguins.

As Pie was leaving the rink with the twins, Terry ran up beside them, grinning broadly and proudly. At his heels was Pam, carrying Tipper.

"Hi," he said.

"Hi," they greeted him.

"Going to play with your hockey game this afternoon?"

The twins looked at Pie, their eyes carrying a secret message. "Shall we, Pie?"

Pie shrugged. "Why not?"

Terry chuckled. "I wonder if . . . well, mind if I came over and played, too?"

Again the twins and Pie exchanged a look. Then Pie winked.

"Of course, you know why he wants to come over and play, don't you?" he said.

"Of course," said Jody. "He wants to see whether the game is really magic."

"Right. Okay, Terry. If it's all right with the twins, it's all right with me."

"Oh, it's all right with us!" replied the twins.

"Thanks!" said Terry, his teeth flashing white as he grinned. "See you guys later! Oh, one more thing. Sorry about your skate, Pie. I hope you'll get a new pair."

"Me, too," Pie replied.

He really wasn't surprised when his father saw the broken skate and said, "No doubt about it now, son. You've got to have a new pair. We'll go to a store together after lunch."

At 1:00 they walked to a store and Mr. Pennelli bought Pie a new pair of skates, one that fit tighter than his regular shoes. Pie was sure that he would never again make a quick turn with his feet moving before his skates did.

At 3:00 Terry showed up at the twins' house. They called Pie over, and all four of them went down to the basement. Terry had his cat with him, which didn't surprise Pie. Those two were practically inseparable.

They reached the table on which the hockey game was set and started to sit down, when suddenly the cat cried, "*Meow!*" and leaped off Terry's shoulder directly onto the game.

He sat there, gazing big-eyed at the miniature hockey figures, until Terry yelled, "Git, Tipper! Where are your manners?"

The cat jumped off.

At the same time something clicked in Pie's mind as he stared at the cat. He looked at the twins, and from their expressions he knew that the same thing had clicked in their minds, too.

Beware what happens on a real rink first
Repeats here not, for fate
Promises that, as true as bubbles burst,
The magic will dissipate.

The cat had done it. He had jumped onto the ice at the rink, and now onto the toy hockey game.

The magic was gone, and deep within him, Pie knew he was glad.

How many of these Matt Christopher sports classics have you read?

- Baseball Pals
- The Basket Counts
- Catch That Pass!
- Catcher with a Glass Arm
- Challenge at Second Base
- The Counterfeit Tackle
- The Diamond Champs
- Dirt Bike Racer
- Dirt Bike Runaway
- Face-Off
- Football Fugitive
- The Fox Steals Home
- The Great Quarterback Switch
- Hard Drive to Short
- The Hockey Machine
- Ice Magic
- Johnny Long Legs
- The Kid Who Only Hit Homers
- Little Lefty
- Long Shot for Paul
- Long Stretch at First Base
- Look Who's Playing First Base
- Miracle at the Plate
- No Arm in Left Field
- Red-Hot Hightops
- Return of the Home Run Kid
- Run, Billy, Run
- Shortstop from Tokyo
- Skateboard Tough
- Soccer Halfback
- The Submarine Pitch
- Supercharged Infield
- Tackle Without a Team
- Tight End
- Too Hot to Handle
- Touchdown for Tommy
- Tough to Tackle
- Undercover Tailback
- Wingman on Ice
- The Year Mom Won the Pennant

All available in paperback from Little, Brown and Company